A NOTE TO PARENTS

When your children are ready to "step into reading," giving them the right books—and lots of them—is as crucial as giving them the right food to eat. **Step into Reading Books** present exciting stories and information reinforced with lively, colorful illustrations that make learning to read fun, satisfying, and worthwhile. They are priced so that acquiring an entire library of them is affordable. And they are beginning readers with an important difference—they're written on four levels.

Step 1 Books, with their very large type and extremely simple vocabulary, have been created for the very youngest readers. **Step 2 Books** are both longer and slightly more difficult. **Step 3 Books,** written to mid-second-grade reading levels, are for the child who has acquired even greater reading skills. **Step 4 Books** offer exciting nonfiction for the increasingly proficient reader.

Children develop at different ages. **Step into Reading Books,** with their four levels of reading, are designed to help children become good—and interested—readers *faster*. The grade levels assigned to the four steps—preschool through grade 1 for Step 1, grades 1 through 3 for Step 2, grades 2 and 3 for Step 3, and grades 2 through 4 for Step 4—are intended only as guides. Some children move through all four steps very rapidly; others climb the steps over a period of several years. These books will help your child "step into reading" in style!

Text copyright © 1992 by Natalie Standiford. Illustrations copyright © 1992 by Donald Cook. All rights reserved under International and Pan-American Copyright Conventions. Published in the United States by Random House, Inc., New York, and simultaneously in Canada by Random House of Canada Limited, Toronto.

Library of Congress Cataloging-in-Publication Data:
Standiford, Natalie. The headless horseman / by Natalie Standiford; illustrated by Donald Cook.
p.   cm.–(Step into reading. A step 2 book) Based on the classic ghost story, The legend of Sleepy Hollow by Washington Irving. Summary: A superstitious schoolmaster, in love with a wealthy farmer's daughter, has a terrifying encounter with a headless horseman. ISBN 0-679-81241-5 (trade) ISBN 0-679-91241-X (lib. bdg.) [1. Ghosts–Fiction. 2. New York (State)–Fiction.] I. Cook, Donald, ill. II. Irving, Washington, 1783–1859. Legend of Sleepy Hollow. III. Title. IV. Series: Step into reading. Step 2 book.   PZ7.S78627He 1992 [E]–dc20 90-53228

Manufactured in the United States of America   25   26   27   28   29   30

STEP INTO READING is a trademark of Random House, Inc.

Step into Reading

The
Headless Horseman

Based on
"The Legend of Sleepy Hollow"
by Washington Irving

Adapted by Natalie Standiford
Illustrated by Donald Cook

A Step 2 Book

Random House 🏠 New York

Once there was a town

called Sleepy Hollow.

It was a drowsy little town

in a pretty green valley.

Life there was always

peaceful and quiet.

But at night

the town was <u>too</u> quiet.

Then you might see something

move in the shadows.

Then you might hear something

moan in the dark.

Then you might believe

Sleepy Hollow was haunted!

The people who lived there

thought the whole valley

was haunted.

They told strange tales

about ghosts and goblins and witches.

The strangest tale of all

was the story of

the Headless Horseman.

"During the war,"

began the story,

"a bloody battle

was fought in the valley.

Swords clashed.

Cannons boomed.

One soldier on horseback

lost his head."

"His headless body was buried
in the church graveyard.
The tombstone reads REST IN PEACE.
But the poor soul buried there
cannot rest...."

"Now, on nights

when the moon is full,

he rises from the grave.

He mounts his phantom horse

and rides through the valley,

looking for his head.

So…

beware the Headless Horseman!

If he cannot find <u>his</u> head,

he will gladly take yours!"

No one believed in ghost stories
more than the schoolteacher,
Ichabod Crane.
He was an odd-looking fellow—
tall and skinny,
with dangling arms
and floppy feet.
When he walked down the street,
he looked just like a scarecrow
off its post.

Ichabod was poor,

but he had a plan.

He was going to marry Katrina Van Tassel.

Her father was the richest squire

in the valley.

Ichabod wanted to be just like him.

Brom Bones also wanted
to marry Katrina.

Brom was a friendly young man.

He liked to play tricks
and ride horses and have fun.

All the young ladies liked him.

Especially Katrina!

Ichabod did his best

to win Katrina's heart.

He read his favorite books to her.

He sang his favorite songs to her.

He told her all about himself.

17

Naturally, Brom Bones was jealous.

So he played a trick on Ichabod.

Late one night

Brom sneaked into the schoolhouse.

He turned the whole place

topsy-turvy.

When Ichabod arrived in the morning,

he was horrified.

Witches must have held

a meeting there!

He was afraid to teach that day.

Then one afternoon

an invitation came.

The Van Tassels

were having a party!

Ichabod jumped for joy.

He sent his pupils home

and started getting ready.

He put on his one and only suit.

He combed his hair.

He borrowed a broken-down horse

and set out for Katrina's house.

The sun was still shining

as he rode along.

It was harvest-time

in the valley.

Everything was golden.

Ichabod whistled a happy tune.

But when he rode into the woods,

the light faded.

Ichabod stopped whistling.

He went over the bridge

and past the church.

Then he saw the church graveyard.

It gave him the shivers.

Ichabod's horse was very slow.

It was already dark

when Ichabod arrived at the party.

Katrina's house was lit up

like the moon.

Someday, thought Ichabod,

all this will be mine.

Then some other poor sap

will be the schoolteacher.

And I won't even invite him

to my parties!

Ichabod went inside.

Katrina was dancing with Brom Bones.

He tapped Brom on the shoulder.

"Ahem," he said. "May I cut in?"

Brom stepped aside

and let Ichabod dance with Katrina.

By and by, Brom tapped Ichabod.

But Ichabod would not step aside.

Instead, he twirled Katrina away.

Brom was angry.

Later that evening

Brom went outside.

An old man was telling ghost stories.

And there was Ichabod—

believing every word!

"I saw the Headless Horseman

just last night," said Brom.

"He raced me for a cup of punch.

I would have won, too.

But as soon

as I crossed the church bridge,

the Headless Horseman vanished

in a flash of fire."

Ichabod's eyes grew wide.

Brom smiled.

Perhaps the Headless Horseman

would ride that very night!

The party was over.

Ichabod was the last to leave.

He was miserable.

He had asked Katrina to marry him.

But she had turned him down.

It was midnight

as he rode toward home.

The woods had never seemed so dark.

An owl hooted.

A frog croaked.

A dog howled in the distance.

Clouds hid the moon.

The woods were darker than ever.

To cheer himself up,

Ichabod began to whistle.

Suddenly...

someone whistled back!

Ichabod looked around.

In the shadows

stood a huge dark shape!

Ichabod's horse stopped dead.

Just then the moon came out

from behind the clouds.

The huge dark shape

began to look like a horse.

On top of the horse sat a man.

On top of the man's shoulders sat—

nothing!

But there was a head

under his arm!

Ichabod screamed.

The Headless Horseman!

Ichabod remembered Brom's story.

If only he could cross

the church bridge!

Then he would be safe.

He kicked his horse.

"Go! Go!" urged Ichabod

in a whisper.

But the horse would not budge.

He kicked his horse again.

Finally, the old horse dashed forward.

The Headless Horseman
dashed forward too.

Away they went—

in a race to the bridge,

Ichabod riding for his life!

Ichabod leaned forward.

Faster, faster!

The horse clattered over the bridge,

with Ichabod clinging to its back.

Was he safe?

Ichabod glanced back.

The Headless Horseman had stopped.

Suddenly his horse reared up.

And with a chilling laugh

the Headless Horseman hurled his head

across the bridge—

right at Ichabod Crane!

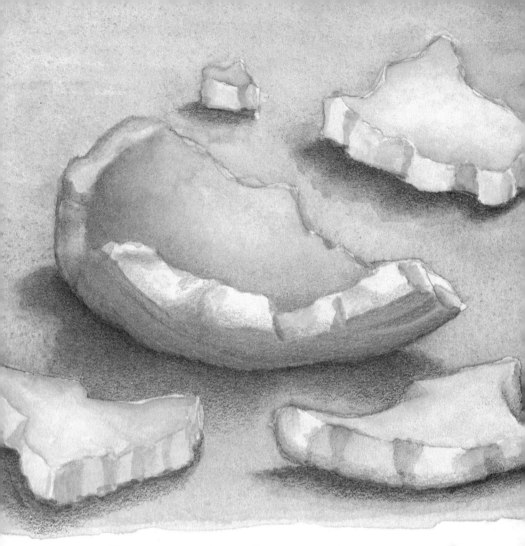

The next morning

Ichabod's horse was found

nibbling grass at the edge of town.

But where was Ichabod Crane?

The people of Sleepy Hollow

set out to look for him.

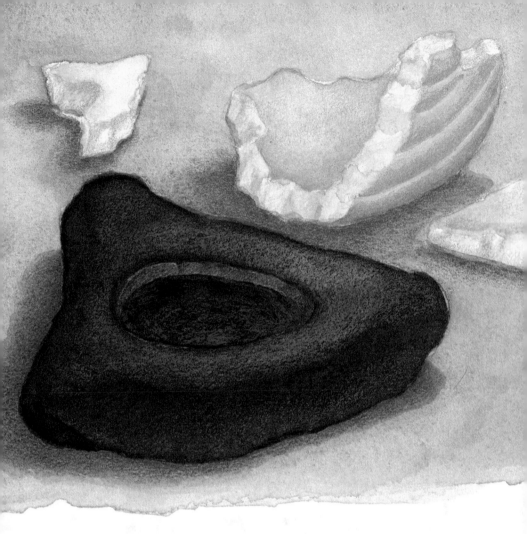

They found his hat

near the church bridge.

They found a smashed pumpkin

next to the hat.

But Ichabod himself

they never found.

People could think of only one reason

for Ichabod's disappearance:

the Headless Horseman had carried him away.

A farmer said he had seen

a man who looked like Ichabod

in another valley far away.

But no one believed him.

Everybody knew that Ichabod's ghost

now haunted the old church bridge.

When Brom Bones heard these stories,

he would get a sneaky look on his face.

If he knew what really happened,

he wasn't telling.